Matilda's Cat

Emily Gravett

Macmillan Children's Books

Matilda's cat likes
playing with wool,

~~playing with wool,~~

boxes,

~~playing with wool,~~
~~boxes,~~
      and riding bikes!

Matilda's cat likes
tea parties,

~~tea parties,~~ funky hats,

~~tea parties,~~
~~funky hats,~~
and fighting foes!

Matilda's cat likes drawing.

~~drawing,~~

climbing trees,

~~drawing,~~
~~climbing trees,~~
and bedtime stories.

Matilda's cat does NOT like
playing with wool,
boxes,
riding bikes,
tea parties,
funky hats,
fighting foes,
drawing,
climbing trees,
OR bedtime stories.

Matilda's cat likes...